MY FIRST BOOK OF

NURSERY
SONGS & RHYMES

Illustrated by Trace Moroney

The Five Mile Press

The Five Mile Press Pty Ltd
1 Centre Road, Scoresby
Victoria 3179 Australia
Email: publishing@fivemile.com.au
Website: www.fivemile.com.au

This format first published 2006
Reprinted 2007, 2008
Illustration copyright © Tracey Moroney
Design and concept copyright © The Five Mile Press Pty Ltd
CD produced by Spoken Word Productions

National Library of Australia Cataloguing-in-Publication data

Moroney, Trace
My first book of nursery songs and rhymes

For children
ISBN 978 1 74178 208 0

1. Nursery rhymes. 2. Children's songs, English. I. Title

398.8

Contents

Hey Diddle, Diddle

Hey diddle, diddle,
The cat and the fiddle,
The cow jumped over the moon.
The little dog laughed
To see such fun,
And the dish ran away with the spoon.

Row, Row, Row Your Boat

Row, row, row your boat,
Gently down the stream,
Merrily, merrily, merrily, merrily,
Life is but a dream.

Baa, Baa, Black Sheep

Baa, baa, black sheep,
Have you any wool?
Yes sir, yes sir,
Three bags full.
One for the master,
One for the dame,
And one for the little boy
Who lives down the lane.

Hush, Little Baby

Hush, little baby, don't say a word,
Poppa's gonna buy you a mockingbird.
And if that mockingbird won't sing,
Poppa's gonna buy you a diamond ring.

And if that diamond ring turns to brass,
Poppa's gonna buy you a looking-glass.
And if that looking-glass gets broke,
Poppa's gonna buy you a billy-goat.
And if that billy-goat won't pull,
Poppa's gonna buy you a cart and bull.

And if that cart and bull turn over,
Poppa's gonna buy you a dog named Rover.
And if that dog named Rover won't bark,
Poppa's gonna buy you a horse and cart.
And if that horse and cart fall down,
You'll still be the sweetest little baby in town!

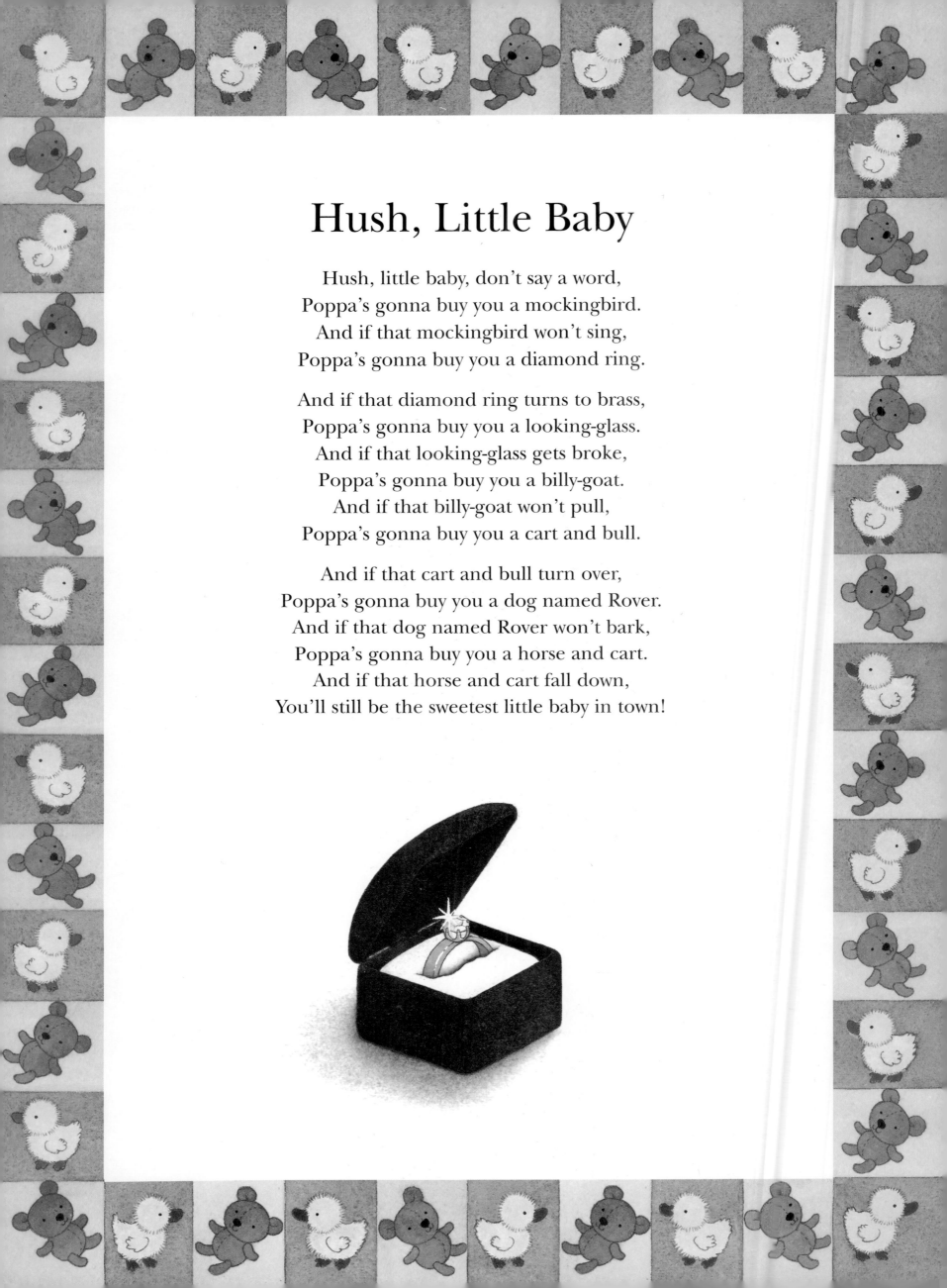

Pussy Cat, Pussy Cat

Pussy cat, pussy cat,
Where have you been?
I've been to London
To look at the queen.
Pussy cat, pussy cat,
What did you there?
I frightened a little mouse
Under her chair.

Ring-a-ring o' Roses

Ring-a-ring o' roses,
A pocket full of posies,
A-tishoo! A-tishoo!
We all fall down!

Three Little Kittens

Three little kittens they lost their mittens,
And they began to cry,
'Oh! Mother dear, we greatly fear
Our mittens we have lost.'

'What! Lost your mittens,
You naughty kittens,
Then you shall have no pie.
Mee-ow, mee-ow, mee-ow.
Then you shall have no pie.'

Twinkle, Twinkle, Little Star

Twinkle, twinkle, little star,
How I wonder what you are,
Up above the world so high,
Like a diamond in the sky.
Twinkle, twinkle, little star,
How I wonder what you are!

Jack and Jill

Jack and Jill went up the hill
To fetch a pail of water.
Jack fell down and broke his crown,
And Jill came tumbling after.

Up Jack got, and home did trot,
As fast as he could caper.
He went to bed to mend his head,
With vinegar and brown paper.

Old MacDonald

Old MacDonald had a farm,
E-I-E-I-O,
And on that farm he had some ducks,
E-I-E-I-O,
With a quack-quack here and a quack-quack there,
Here a quack, there a quack, everywhere a quack-quack.
Old MacDonald had a farm,
E-I-E-I-O.

Old MacDonald had a farm,
E-I-E-I-O,
And on that farm he had some cows,
E-I-E-I-O,
With a moo-moo here and a moo-moo there,
Here a moo, there a moo, everywhere a moo-moo.
E-I-E-I-O.

It's Raining, It's Pouring

It's raining, it's pouring,
The old man's snoring,
He bumped his head
Upon the bed,
And he couldn't get up in the morning.

The Wheels on the Bus

The wheels on the bus go round and round,
Round and round, round and round!
The wheels on the bus go round and round,
All over town.

The doors on the bus swing open and shut,
Open and shut, open and shut!
The doors on the bus swing open and shut,
All over town.

The wiper on the bus goes swish, swish, swish,
Swish, swish, swish,
Swish, swish, swish!
The wiper on the bus goes
Swish, swish, swish,
All over town.